Baseball

• An Introduction to Being a Good Sport •

by Aaron Derr
illustrations by Scott Angle

RED
CHAIR
PRESS™

Start Smart books are published by Red Chair Press

Red Chair Press LLC   PO Box 333   South Egremont, MA 01258-0333

www.redchairpress.com

Publisher's Cataloging-In-Publication Data

Names: Derr, Aaron. | Angle, Scott, illustrator.

Title: Baseball : an introduction to being a good sport / by Aaron Derr ; illustrations by Scott Angle.

Description: South Egremont, MA : Red Chair Press, [2017] | Start smart: sports | Interest age level: 005-009. | Includes Fast Fact sidebars, a glossary and references for additional reading. | Includes bibliographical references and index. | Summary: "Playing a sport is good exercise and fun, but being part of a team is more fun for everyone when you know the rules of the game and how to be a good sport. Baseball is one of the most popular team sports in North America and the Caribbean nations. In this book, readers learn the history of the game and the role of various positions in the field."-- Provided by publisher.

Identifiers: LCCN 2016934113 | ISBN 978-1-63440-129-6 (library hardcover) | ISBN 978-1-63440-135-7 (paperback) | ISBN 978-1-63440-141-8 (ebook)

Subjects: LCSH: Baseball--Juvenile literature. | Sportsmanship--Juvenile literature. CYAC: Baseball. | Sportsmanship.

Classification: LCC GV867.5 .D47 2017 (print) | LCC GV867.5 (ebook) | DDC 796.357--dc23

Illustration credits: Scott Angle; technical charts by Joe LeMonnier

Photo credits: Cover p. 8, 10, 13, 15, 22, 27, 29, 30, 32: Shutterstock; p. 32: Courtesy of the author, Aaron Derr

This series first published by:
Red Chair Press LLC   PO Box 333   South Egremont, MA 01258-0333

Printed in the United States of America

Distributed in the U.S. by Lerner Publisher Services. www.lernerbooks.com

1116 1P CGBS17

Table of Contents

Words in **bold type** are defined in the glossary.

CHAPTER 1

Game Day

Ethan's alarm clock goes off at 8 a.m. But Ethan is already awake! He is excited because today is the first day of baseball season. And he has to start getting ready for the game.

"Mom! Dad! It's time to go!" Ethan says after eating breakfast and putting on his uniform. Ethan is part of a team. He plays for the Tigers, and all of his teammates wear the same uniform, except for the numbers on the back.

Most of his teammates are friends. They help each other out if one of them makes a mistake. And if one of them does well, they slap high-fives and pat each other on the back.

Ethan loves being part of a team. And on this morning, his teammates need him to get to the ballpark and get ready to play ball!

FUN FACT

The first official rules of baseball were written in 1845. That's more than 170 years ago!

CHAPTER 2

Taking the Field

Ethan gets to the baseball field, the first person he sees is his baseball coach. Ethan likes Coach Jones. He always tells Ethan what to do to help the team win.

"Hi Ethan! Are you ready to have a great game?" Coach Jones asks. "Yes, coach! I'm ready," Ethan says.

JUST JOKING!

Q: What animal makes the best baseball player?

A: A bat!

Ethan runs into the **dugout** to check out the lineup card. It tells him and his teammates what **positions** they will play in this game. It also shows them the **batting order**.

Ethan looks at the lineup card and sees that he's playing **first base**. "Yes!" he says. "I love playing first base!"

In baseball, one team bats, while the other is in the field. The batters try to hit the ball as hard as they can, and the fielders try to catch it. If the fielder catches the ball before it hits the ground, the batter is out!

If the fielder can't get to the ball before it bounces, the batter gets to run to first base. If the fielder still doesn't have the ball, the batter can try for second base, or third base, or even **home plate**. If the batter makes it all the way home, he scores a **run**.

FUN FACT

Baseball players wear gloves to help them catch the ball. If you're right-handed, you'll wear your glove on your left hand. If you throw with your left hand, your glove goes on your right.

But the batter has to be careful! If one of the fielders gets the ball and **tags** him before he gets to a base, he's out. Then he has to go back to the dugout. Sometimes it's best to stay on the base so you can't be tagged out.

Runners can also be called out on a play called a "force out." Let's say the batter hits the ball on the ground. If the fielder with the ball can touch first base before the batter gets there, the batter is out! It's called a "force" play because the batter is "forced" to run to first base. If there is already a runner on first base, the fielders can get a force out at second base and first base. You can get force outs at any base when the runner is "forced" to try to run to the next base.

It's up to the fielders to use teamwork to keep the batter from getting too far. When a fielder gets the ball, he can throw it to a teammate that is close to the runner. If the teammate can't tag the runner out, he can at least keep him from going to the next base.

IN THE FIELD!

On a baseball field, players are in their positions as shown here.

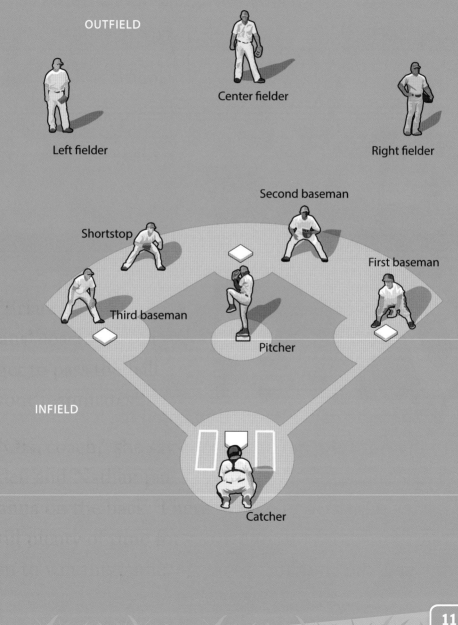

OUTFIELD

Center fielder

Left fielder

Right fielder

Second baseman

Shortstop

First baseman

Third baseman

Pitcher

INFIELD

Catcher

Batter Up

When the game starts, Ethan and his teammates run to the **outfield** and **infield** and take their positions. Their coach tells them to get "baseball ready." That means they have to pay close attention to the batter. If one of them isn't paying attention and the batter hits the ball, they might miss it.

Crack! The first batter of the game swings and hits the ball right at Ethan. He tries to catch it. But the ball bounces off his glove and hits the ground. The batter is **safe** at first base.

Ethan feels bad that he didn't catch the ball. But the feeling doesn't last long.

"That's OK, Ethan!" says his teammate Erin from third base.

"Nice try, Ethan! You'll get it next time!" says his teammate Lucas from the outfield.

FUN FACT

Professional baseball players use bats made of wood. Most kids use bats made of metal.

This makes Ethan feel better. And it's a good thing, because … crack! The next batter hits the ball to Ethan, too. This time Ethan makes the catch. The batter is out!

"Great catch, Ethan!" says Jenny at second base.

"Good job, Ethan!" says Billy at **shortstop**.

Baseball doesn't have a clock like soccer or basketball. Instead, baseball has innings. You have to get three outs before the inning is over, and the Tigers have only gotten one out so far.

DID YOU KNOW?

The balls used in baseball have something called a cork in the center. The cork is wrapped in yarn and covered with leather.

Crack! The next batter hits the ball right to Jenny. It bounces before it gets to her, so she has to pick it up and tag the runner before he gets to the next base. He's out!

Crack! The next batter hits the ball to Johnny in the outfield. He can't catch it, but he can throw the ball to Erin. She catches the throw and tags the runner. He's out! The inning is over, and now it's the Tigers' turn to bat.

CHAPTER 4

Doing Your Best

When the Tigers are batting, one player stands at the plate and the rest wait their turn. While they're waiting in the dugout, Ethan and his teammates cheer on the batter.

"Go Tigers!" they all say.

Once the batter hits the ball, it's a good idea to run as fast as you can to first base, even if it looks like you're going to be out. You never know when the other team might drop the ball or make a bad throw.

Erin is the first batter of the game. She's one of the Tigers' best players. She swings hard at the ball. That's because Erin tries her best and she always has a good attitude.

JUST JOKING!

Q: Where does a baseball player go when he needs a new uniform?

A: New Jersey!

N.J.

When the first **pitch** comes in, Erin swings as hard as she can, but she misses the ball. That's called a strike. If you get three strikes, you're out.

When the second pitch comes in, Erin misses again. If she gets one more strike, she'll be out.

When the third pitch comes in, Erin thinks for sure she will hit this one. She swings as hard as she can, but she misses again. Erin is out. She walks back to the dugout feeling sad.

"That's OK, Erin," Ethan says. "You'll hit it next time for sure!"

"Great try, Erin," says Freddy. "You almost got it."

Erin smiles. She loves being part of a team, just like Ethan.

FUN FACT

Teams in Major League Baseball are split into two leagues: 15 in the American League and 15 in the National League. These are the best baseball players. There are also more than 200 minor league teams. These players are very good but are not quite ready for the majors.

In baseball, stealing is OK! A runner can try to run to the next base at any time. If he makes it, it's called a stolen base. But he has to be careful. As soon as leaves the base, the fielders can tag him out. Better run fast!

The next batter, Billy, swings and hits the ball so hard that he makes it all the way to second base. Great hit! Billy thinks about trying to get to third base. But the other team has the ball, and they might tag him out. So he stays at second.

Now it's Ethan's turn to bat. His teammates need him to get a hit so Billy can try to score. On the first pitch, Ethan swings and misses. Strike one. On the second pitch, Ethan swings and misses again. Strike two.

"Come on Ethan, you can do it!" yells Johnny.

"Go Ethan! Hit that ball!" says Erin.

And on the next pitch, Ethan gets a hit! While he's running as fast as he can to first base, Billy is running to third base. But the ball is still going! So Ethan goes to second base, and Billy goes to home plate. The Tigers have scored a run!

DID YOU KNOW?

At the end of the season, the best team from the American League plays against the best team in the National League. This is called the World Series. The winner is the champion for that season.

CHAPTER 5

Game Over

Major League Baseball games last nine innings, but most kids only play five or seven innings. Then the game is over … unless the score is tied! If both teams have the same number of runs, they play extra innings until one team has more runs than the other.

The Tigers play a great game today. They score lots of runs, but the players on the other team are trying their best, too. The coaches cheer for their players. The moms and dads watching in the **stands** cheer even louder.

In the end, the other team has more runs, and the Tigers have lost the game. They walk onto the field and shake hands with the players from the other team.

"Good game," the Tigers' players say.

"You guys played great," say the players from the other team.

JUST JOKING!

Q: Why did the baseball player go to jail?

A: For stealing second base!

Ethan and his teammates feel sad, but Coach Jones makes everybody feel better. He calls all of his players around him and tells them how proud he is.

"You guys did great!" Coach says. "You tried your best, and that's all I ever ask."

By the time Ethan gets home, he's already thinking about the next game.

"I love being on a team," he says.

The only way to become a good baseball player is to practice. Start by playing catch with a friend or trusted adult. Don't try to throw the ball hard. Just try to throw it straight at your friend every time.

When you're learning how to catch, don't be afraid of the ball! That hard ball won't hurt you as long as you keep you eyes on it.

Learning to hit is trickier. Most kids start by hitting off a **tee**. Once you get the hang of that, have a friend throw slow pitches for you to hit.

Remember: Baseball bats are heavy. Baseballs are hard. Both can break windows, so always play in a safe area. Be careful and follow the rules.

Glossary

batting order: the order in which batters take their turn

dugout: a row of seats at the side of a baseball field where a team's coaches and players can watch the game

first base: the first place a batter runs after hitting the ball

home plate: the base that a batter stands next to when hitting and also the last one he/she must touch after running to all of the other bases

infield: the area near the four bases where the first baseman, second baseman, shortstop and third baseman play

outfield: the players who stand the farthest away from home plate to catch long balls

pitch: the throwing of the ball by the pitcher that the batter tries to swing at it

positions: the place where the fielders are put

professional: a person who gets paid to play baseball as a full-time job

run: a point score when a runner safely touches home plate

safe: when a runner makes it to the next base without being tagged or forced out

shortstop: the fielder that plays between third base and second base

stands: a place for fans to watch the game

tag: the act of touching a runner with the ball and putting him out

tee: a small stand used to hold a baseball before it is hit

What Did You Learn?

See how much you learned about baseball. Answer *true* or *false* for each statement below. Write your answers on a separate piece of paper.

1 If a fielder catches a batted ball on one hop, the batter is out. True or false?

2 In baseball, points are called runs. True or false?

3 Baseball teams use four infielders. True or false?

4 Innings are finished after 15 minutes. True or false?

5 Major League Baseball is divided into two leagues: the East and the West. True or false?

For More Information

Books

Braun, Eric. *Super Baseball Infographics.* Lerner Publishing, 2015.

Dreier, David. *Baseball: How It Works* (SI for Kids). Capstone Press, 2010.

Editors, SI for Kids. *Full Count: The Top 10 Lists of Everything in Baseball.* Sports Illustrated Books, 2012.

Jacobs, Greg. *The Everything Kids' Baseball Book, 8th Edition.* Adams Media, 2014.

Places

National Baseball Hall of Fame, Cooperstown, New York. Loads of history about the sport plus over 40,000 items such as baseball cards and players' gear.

Fenway Park, Boston, Massachusetts. America's oldest major league ballpark is still home for MLB's Red Sox. Built in 1912.

Louisville Slugger Museum and Factory, Louisville, Kentucky. Making baseball bats since 1884.

Web Sites

Games, data and coaching videos for kids.
www.baseballrox.com

Official site of Major League Baseball with links to every team's kids' pages.
www.mlb.mlb.com/kids

Note to educators and parents: Our editors have carefully reviewed these web sites to ensure they are suitable for children. Web sites change frequently, however, and we cannot guarantee that a site's future contents will continue to meet our high standards of quality and educational value. You may wish to preview these sites and closely supervise children whenever they access the Internet.

Index

About the Author

Aaron Derr Aaron Derr is a writer based just outside of Dallas, Texas. He has more than 15 years of experience writing and editing magazines and books for kids of all ages. When he's not reading or writing, Aaron enjoys watching and playing sports, and being a good sport with his wife and two kids.